I was expecting someone taller

Dear Joan:
Your support
means a lot!
Thanks!

I WAS EXPECTING
SOMEONE TALLER

SUE NEVILL

Sue Nevill

A Porcépic Book
BEACH HOLME PUBLISHING LIMITED

Victoria

This edition is published by Beach Holme Publishers Limited,
4252 Commerce Circle, Victoria, B.C., V8Z 4M2, with the assist-
ance of the Canada Council and the B.C. Ministry of Municipal
Affairs, Recreation and Culture. This is a Porcépic Book.

Cover Design by Christine Toller
Production Editor: Antonia Banyard
Cover art: "Charger" by Robert Youds (from a private collection)

Canadian Cataloguing in Publication Data
    Nevill, Sue, 1944-
      I was expecting someone taller

      Poems.
      ISBN 0-88878-311-6

      I. Title
PS8577.E9412 1991   C811'.54   C91-091555-5
PR9199.3.N4812 1991

To my friends, with gratitude for your
lively minds, open hearts and endless patience.

snap

street people freezing

castanets in human clothes they
jitter forward   cuddle up to cars
burn their hands on frigid
garbage cans

blue faces strain toward the lights
like grounded moths   fingers search
thin pockets for grains of heat
tremble for spare change

a jostle splinters them snaps
their legs off just above their
toe-turned cowboy boots   their pieces
shatter on the pavement
broken ice along a broken street

impact

thinking of you
I drive into
a parked
police car

jeez lady   snarls the
cop   snatching at
my licence
you under the
influence or what

why yes   I say
surprised
how did you know

three hours later
they still don't
understand about love

Weedeater.

I can see how a person
might get carried away,
mesmerized by supernatural
circles, the whir of line—crisp,
invisible—reducing perennial invaders
to tidy stubble in the space of one leisurely
grass-sweet stroll:
first the high tufted dandelions
along the fence bottom, hollow stems
yielding like soft butter; on to the
shag-encircled cedar roots, shaving round
them with a whine no louder than a pack of
decent-sized mosquitoes, here and there a smack
against the knobby wood as satisfying as the chunk
of well-swung summer bats.

The upright comfort of it,
the giddy freedom from screaming
knees. The smoothness. The triumph of order
easily attained.

Then turning to survey the clovered lawn;
the boulevard of pushy plantain spears; the
neighbour's yard with its unneighbourly burst of
chickweed: all absorbed with one elated breath
of painless, practically silent, possibility.

And after this street, the next.

suspicious packages

veteran shoppers
retreat a token metre
from plate glass
windows stretch for
a better view of
the bomb squad

police must push
the people to defend them
from the 2:30 bus
to tel aviv which may be
going somewhere else
this trip

and i am with these crowds
share their compulsion
to see ends clearly

it is imperative to feel
how tall death is
to taste the colour of his
hair as he strides
toward us

i think she died of joy*

*(comment by a friend of
Josephine Baker, on Baker's
death after a triumphant
return to the Paris stage.)

j'ai deux amours she sang
danced brown and naked for
an age of lovers who took
her with their eyes
laid her out
on canvas   massaged her
into metal

picasso calder daumier
quick twists of paint
and ink   slashes of hot bronze
tried to catch
the sun in a black net
stocking
she was too quick
for them   rainbows
of sweat reminded them
of just where she had been
last time they looked

she melted stages
moved
to freedom   took
her watchers with her
into flight as far
as they could
follow

feathers   castles
medals   none as dazzling
as her own polished skin
from behind the masks
her wicked grin hung
on like the alice cat's

she died
in satisfying parisian
fashion   partying
at an ageless age
to good reviews

i think she died
of joy

rerun

i am watching
the same television
show i watched 20 years
ago today it is colour
enhanced
like any
good memory
the sets are
gold this time
not cardboard
and i nod my
approval yes
that's the way
it really was
the actors
are terrific
i wonder
why this show
went off
the air

this is drama
this is art

i nod and laugh
and cry
forget the bad reviews
we shouted at
each other

express lane

sun flares round the window banners
all winter we believed this supermarket glass
was tinted   now we recognize its film
as january fingerprints
february breath

under the 8 items cash only sign
the fastest checker in the store
forces her arms through lemonbutter light
rings up 12 items
takes a cheque

no one complains
no one shifts from foot
to foot or flips through
national enquirer
the sun has frozen us in line
stunned us with the possiblity
of sudden gifts
bottled cranberry juice becomes a
giant ruby
we blink in satisfaction
stare at the chocolate bars
hoping for a spring-confirming melt

the checker fills another bag
the corners of her mouth are
too relaxed for smiling
her arms drop to her sides
she turns her face into the sun
closes her eyes and
yawns

SUE NEVILL

icehouse

where to step from
bed is to wake up
through the soles
completely

shrinking
i skate toward the
toilet hating consciousness
resisting sight   grey early
light had pried the
bathroom window open
prepared the shivering towels
and toilet seat for dew
the tiles are cakes
of coloured ice   i
freeze to walls   i
leave behind the patches
of my skin not already frozen
fast to you

in your bathroom
in your bed
these days no great difference
in temperature

all-star café

jesus and i do lunch
fish and a little wine
lots of quotable
quotes   i was expecting
someone taller

he introduces me to
his old man   yahweh's
in the demolition business
never off his
portable phone

the guy at the next table
keeps fooling with his
walkman looks like
he's getting static
mohammed   j.c. says and
shrugs

in the corner booth
two hairdos i recognize
marx and lenin
sharing one workers'
daily special   arguing over
who gets the bread

these heavy hitters
they're o.k. when you get
to know them   it's the groupies
that make a person puke

greyhound

oh i was as scared as the next
man alright   8 fuckin hours
on that bloody bus with
some weird arab type wavin
a gun around   i mean
this is *canada* for crissake
not one a those bareass
countries where they hijack
everything that moves

hard to believe the guy
was serious   specially
when he tells the driver
take me to ottawa

except for the gun i
would of laughed

lotsa luck buddy
i would of said
lotsa fuckin luck

no place like

keep moving
hips like rusty gates today
legs like shaky stilts and canes no help
at 81 you have to keep on moving   can't let
your daughter see you wincing trembling
that home she talks about well that's
no place for me   no room for
mother's hutch my wedding suite Bill's paintings
heart pounds so loud it hurts   oh
                        talk to her now
tell her something   Mrs. Jacobs' new azalea   cats
dug up the tulip bulbs no I think I told her that
already
where did I put the bills   don't let
her see you searching   *did* I
already tell her
              hide the broken plate
and keep on moving can't sit down
it's a lot of trouble getting up these days
sometimes almost
too much trouble but can't sit there forever

stop moving and she'll move me out
                 that home's no place
for me no place at all   those old people
sitting staring giving up
keep moving keep those joints working bones
grinding biting on each other
no I don't need any
help dear

now what's she looking at the nosy girl
those prying ways that's her father's family
doctor's appointment   no that's tomorrow
not today   I'm sure it is tomorrow
oh
well I was just so busy
anybody could forget a thing like that anybody
could forget   I'll phone and   no   let me
I'll do it   heart hurts   this is my house
my house

martha behind the dance

(to Martha Graham)

round eyed caricatures of men
slap flexed feet
show off to
shimmering medea who
is an oscillating
needle of well designed
obsidian
hate

the snake
meanwhile
platinum with malice
is wreathing
their smug ankles
bulging thighs
begging them to
consider falling
now

in the wings
creator
hair severely black
and utterly obedient
her profile slices through
the dusty light toward
stage centre

age she finds amusing
an adequate disguise
for strong
magic
comfort for those who want her
to be mortal

SUE NEVILL

Lindow Man II

even the hair
survives
the face a sagging
agony
skin flows
in leather
rivulets
across his chest
pooling
where it meets
the peat

rubber man
melting
through the centuries
toward us
his opened throat
a second rictus
two grins of
triumph and
conviction:

that his gods
approved
his passing
that all the
rituals
were carried out
correctly
that he died
for all the
right
reasons

British Museum, 1989

passage

(for Clélie)

this flight
this journey alone to meet a man
who has already left
without you

odd to begin the recollection
of his life and yours
in this sealed tube whose mirror windows
keep out the breadth of universe he is
now part of
windows which become the rectangles
inside a family album   showing
his remembered face in sunlight
or under mellow lamps in
well-lived rooms
his image teared and slightly
out of focus
but real enough

more real than this journey
will ever be to you
this flight toward a particular loss
this particular passage you will never
make again
except perhaps in words

epitaph

my uncle died and
and everybody said:
    what a *good* driver he was!

your driving hands

your driving hands
professionally set at
ten to two on the chunky
wheel   pushing into
fast curves   pulling
gliding up and out
one eye on the tach
finesse   control
these crimp the corners of
your mouth   faint
external signs of what
in you
is joy

your fingers on the
gear shift   stroking
sensing   open for
the vibes that tell
you clearly what the
next right move is
do it *now*   explicit

shifting into overdrive on a long
straight stretch you think wishfully
of women as they could be
                        easy to lubricate   tight responsive
steering   systems thoroughly described
in the owner's manual
enough power to excite without the constant danger
of overheating

fellow travellers

where in my world do they
all come from
                    trailing
bags prepacked with monstrous
preconceptions
accepting surfaces as
souvenirs
                    eyes locked
tight behind their shades
against a different light
mouths shut fast and
grim against the smiles
of those who must be
strangers

SHOOTING SCRIPT

OPEN WITH CRANE SHOT. SLOW ZOOM TO waif at a window
thin in the face of the city   stunned under its lights.
5 COUNT mouth opens. Its speech would be a howl
—no too full. Its speech would be a thin scream
squeezed from a core of silence: sharp enough to
score the window glass craze it into webs.
CU famined face—steel cheekbones shellac eyes
LIGHTS UP ON carved stretched lines at eye corners.
Throat cords strum as scream goes on. XCU open mouth
tongue blistered straining from its roots ANGLE DOWN TO
hands playing window sill like a piano   scrabbling
sliding through the dust dead flies   stopping bony
fingers pressing till nails pale on scabby wood.

CAMERA PULLS BACK slow revelation of a suicidal room
falling on itself: mottled paper ceiling   damp
rorschach walls. On the floor the detritus of people
who own nothing not even bodies any more which sprawl
surrendered vacant on thin bare lino   bodies that could
not be walked and talked one second longer even for the
child.

HOLD on child with bodies BKGRND   TOP LITE AT ANGLE
for contrast. MUSIC UP.

SHOOT IN BLACK AND WHITE.

lit crit

stuffing
rivers into
boxes

explaining sky
to a
bird

running on empty

some split second some
1 a.m. when
the pukebrown terry tablecloth couldn't sop up
one more overflow of foam
when most of the women
including yours had tottered home
licking nicotine fingers cut
on a dozen beersworth of broken
promises
        there had to be a moment
when your gut surged when you came
within a coin-flip of punching through
that psychedelic rainbow jukebox if it played
you picked a fine to leave
me lucille just one more
time
       when your eyelids
lifted a fraction higher
than usual for that close to closing
and maybe you couldn't put a fast name
to the man in that bar mirror but
remembered not liking him
all that much
and your
       best buddies
the ones who always hung in there down to the last
beer as long as you were paying
sounded for just one minute
like crows

it probably happened
too fast for you to hold it
you know how these things go one blink
and you can miss them
one blink that's all
you get one chance and then
you're down
          under an avalanche
          of empties.

sproing

(for Aug)

baryshinikov
in town
two performances only
how was it i
asked my friend who
went the first night

well   he said
the whole troupe
danced around for
maybe 3/4 of an hour then
big b hit the stage
in pirate gear
went leap leap
sproing sproing
leap leap leap
sproing
and then went off
and that was the
first half

in the second half
he said
the company
danced around
for oh say 47 minutes
then mikhail baby
flew onstage went
leap leap leap
sproing sproing sproing
leap sproing leap
leap leap
and left

i figure   he said
in a calculating
manner   the ticket
price works out at
roughly 5 bucks a
sproing

which is okay
if you like that
sort of thing
tights and
bulgy crotches I mean

Aftertaste.

I found an old Feiffer cartoon
in my desk last night
stapled to the last letter I ever had
from you.

It shows a woman flooding her couch
with Feiffer tears
for her rejecting lover (you know
he left her from the smug
face in the balloon
above her head).

Halfway through the panel
she dries her tears and grabs
a bottle of wine   fierce
(you can tell) in her determination
to drink his image down to
manageable size

(and I did that
I remember now can even taste
the cheap Bulgarian headache red).

But she can't get the cork out
without him.

Corks
were his job.

(In the cartoon she doesn't
break the neck as I
did trying to push that cork through
pushing pushing swearing sobbing
         damned if I'd let you get away
with this your absence cheating me of a
grand gesture a proper
conclusion   and I drank that red vinegar
glass slivers and all the whole
bloody bottle and hated you for
the length of a hangover.)

Humour here floats up
like bits of bitter cork.

Women who see the cartoon
laugh and then
are quiet
for an appreciable length of time.

foreigner

stranger   the woman
who doesn't understand
the language
walking one yard apart
from your partner

your smile is fixed
he chatters to his (male)
companion   you suspect
they are talking about
you

sometimes
he remembers you   flicks you
an abstracted look or
stares   hard and
surprised to find you there
plunges back into his own
words

leaving you in what
will always be your place

foreigner

centennial

this is the silence of deep old age
a clock ticking in an insulated room
the scrape of unsteady knives on
clumsy ironstone
the body noises you have become deaf
to avoid   these
and the polite ghosts of grown children

this is the time of shrinking
into a dense kernal of self
the throbbing in your left foot
the tremor in your eyelid
make up the evening news

sinking is in order now
into your chair your bed your memories
you are not convinced that you believe
in resurrection

silence should soothe
but there is something wrong with
this one   cold and heavy it contains
a mist of dread that soaks your
clothes at odd moments

they change you   pat your hand
give you extra socks and go away
but you are not sure you want to be left alone
with this particular version of yourself
it is not the one
you expected to find behind the door
of this last small room and
you are uneasy

it whispers to you through your hearing aid
you fear it has done some grievous wrong
some time ago   many years ago   too long
to remember clearly

but this is what remains after a century
of bowel movements   of children
noticed in passing   interests chased
to exhaustion at whatever cost
of never loving anyone who did not do exactly
what you wanted

these silences
this self
this deep short
time

The poet's wife.

Always,
he met you with the air
of a man listening

to private music, to
secret voices overheard.
When he remembered you,

it was with quick
pity and a burst
of sudden speech.

The flick of a bird's wing
was enough to interrupt
his conversation.

I cannot tell you how
irritating this was
to live with.

People called him poet.
I never saw him write
a word.

call me roxy

yo cyrano   kinky in those thigh-high
boots   leather dressed with words and of course
the nose

you dog you
shaking that white plume telling all those
ruffians where to put their rapiers
nose like a finger in their faces

the nose with heart the bursting
brain under the silly hat
and here I am crying in front of
this tv set hard done by
when it comes to centuries I could
have been born in cyrano
while you rack up points in
lutesful of the good old
multisyllables
            devotion   loyalty   all that stuff

the sword is neat too

but it's the highflying blizzards of tossed rosebud
words that get me   wit at the speed of
light that turns me on

wit and the words and
the personal ghost that gives
them shape like a cat under a bedspread

yes I could just do with a loving
snappy acrobat of the mind

faces   who remembers faces after
a year or two   it's the epigrams
that stick to the walls

cyrano you toe-curler   you made it
the right libretto with the right
score everytime

what's a nose
between friends

short cuts

how do you
do she says he says
hi and pleased to
meet you

where do you keep your
knives she says
how soon can i expect
to see them   are you
into sex in the afternoon
and how long will you hold me
after   which part of me do you
want to change first
i love your eyes and your
small neat feet will you
pay my rent

he says what flavours do
your poisons come in   i'm a
leg man myself but your
breasts will do how warmly
will you lie to keep me happy
does your mother call you much
are you going to let me
cry   how do you really feel
about whipped cream and
ice cubes

beer she says
actually he says i'd rather
have some tea
i'll take your arm she
says he says
is that all

SUE NEVILL

quietus

there is no-one here
no reason to stand upright
she sags   shrinks into
a stranger

clothes she can no longer wear
or bear to look at
hang as they were taken off
soiled by specks of cemetery mud

she does not look in mirrors
would not recognize herself
and anyway she is
too busy   so much of him
to remember
she forgets to eat
food spoils in lonely portions

one day she lets
her mother's clock
run
down

somewhat blonde

this woman is
somewhat blonde
tall to the rafters
trembles after
a drink or two
falls upstairs
frequently

this woman bends
under fire
takes good care of
her age   weighs
less than she was
born with

flying has been hard
she never really got the
hang of it   but soon
she will   soon
she will be blonde
to the core   and smiling
will be no trouble   no trouble
at all

exits

men leave

they pack up the canary
and the coltrane tapes
and go   they drown themselves
in television sets or
sneak away to death and
blondes

men keep their mirrors
in inside jacket pockets
buy bic razors by the gross
and stash them in
strategic places
they leave so
smoothly you can hardly
stand it
leave you staring at the empty
toothbrush holder   the old jocky shorts
you use to polish shoes

after the funeral   after
the living room is cut
in half
you have to pinch yourself
you have to hear your voice
bouncing off bare absence
to realize they were never
really there
at all.

after hours

roughed up
satin from the sax

bass foot steps on tight black gravel

piano plays rain on a hot
tin roof somewhere
south

and the voice weaves
the breaths behind the beats the spaces in be
tween
where do
where do the
the notes
go notes go go
where dooo wah

and we all fall
into the spaces we shake
icecubes off beat
our smoke is the mute on the belldark
sound
hot smoky music
the players sweat it down

between the notes
between deep belly breaths
foot lights fog up with their blood why don't they
die when their hearts leap out
like that   why don't
they die their lungs sucked
into horns and saxes
slipping to the floor in
sacks of burned-up notes
why don't
the spots
just burst from clear top voices needling
the ceiling

ahweep ahweep
singer and the sax get married
ey yey eyah looawah who
can tell which voice is which
they can't they don't
want to

on off nights someone grabs this music from our
unmarked doorways scrubs it takes it to rooms with
sunset windows rooms with flowers on clean tables

it comes right back
it runs away with
itself   homes in
on the shadows between the notes
chords that start from a scream in the dark and just go
on

pressure points

if i turn
so

lie on
this side

will it ease the particular
pressure
bone on nerve
constricted vein   cramped
muscle   whatever it
is that makes me
think of you
now

no

even on
this side   even with
eyes closed
tears
the hollow heartbeat
that belongs to
you gone

i turn again

on both sides of
this uneasy body
uneasy bed
your absence presses
harder than ever

how it looks from the
u. of montreal engineering faculty

we have our uses

in sleazy scarlet or white habits
blood splashed from sudden wounds or
hidden on a monthly basis we make
great symbols

calling the earth mother gives its rape
a certain tang
mary knew her place thank god and pedestals
are useful
they hide
the cracks in walls
and everything is eve's fault anyway

alive we are for copulation
absolution procreation
execution
at the hands of any man who finds us
easier to handle when we're
dead

December 6, 1989

cold war

so this
is what licence to love has
made of us   these years
of freedom to be wounded by
surprising strangers
as often as we choose

two old dogs
we sniff around each
other for alien scents
hidden weapons   the last
bewildering bite fresh
in our nerves

if we could we'd burst
through twenty years of
scar tissue   rush together
brushing minds in one
great unconsidered fall
to unknown heights

but look at us

keeping hands and other parts
to ourselves

keeping the distance
of experience

imprints

these are the stories we can write
with our eyes closed with our bare
hearts tied behind
our backs

he left me on the corner and i
never saw a hair of him
again he left me after
med school   he left
me with two children
no money   he just left

words traced out on
gritty panes
of red city mornings

later in the day
rain pours in through unhealed windows
stains our thin curtains

mandance

grace in alleys heaving
garbage   turn and
bend and lift and
follow
through

mandancing legs
rocks and
springs
swift
recoveries balanced on two
toes and the wish
        not to appear
        ridiculous

joy of it   to be a ribbon
anytime he wants to
a ribbon waving curling
snapping back
the grin of neat
svelte
motion   (looks like running silk
                at the time)

joy of it
        watching him
        unfold

in loco parentis

I am not ready yet to see my father naked
perched on the shower seat
like some great featherless angel
bones protruding
muscles lax and undefined
strength fled

nor am I prepared to see
my mother in white rooms
blood their only decoration
wires of pain clenched in her hands

unready   unprepared
denying them their age
I find their vestments fit me strangely
I am not grown enough to be
the mother/father   looker-after   wiper-up

and fear convinces me
there is no time that will not be
too soon

Acknowledgements

Thanks to the CACANADADADA PRESS anthology, *Light Like a Summons*, *Queen's Quarterly*, *The Antigonish Review*, and *The New Quarterly* for publishing many of the poems in this book.

Special thanks to Eileen Kernaghan, and to the Burnaby Writers' Society — both constant sources of support and instruction.